Baby's First Days

Place Photo Here

Welcome to

Written by

Helen Foster James

the World

Illustrated by

Petra Brown

Hello, my little sweetheart —

I'm oh, so glad you're here.

Welcome to the world.

Waking up with sleepy yawns.
Morning's here and day begins.

Hello, sunshine.

Looking out with sparkling eyes.
Happy face and button nose.

Hello, smiley.

Hugging all your fuzzy friends.
Cuddly soft and plushy toys.

Hello, cutie.

Singing songs to make you smile.
Merry notes and singsong fun.
Hello, giggles.

Swinging arms and waving hands.
Happy beat and dancing feet.
Hello, wiggles.

Feeling warm in sunshine beams.
Feathered wings and breezy winds.

Hello, birdie.

Hiding eyes then take a peek.
Funny face and goofy grins.

Hello, silly.

Splashing time in soapy bath.
Sudsy foam and squeaky clean.

Hello, bubbles.

Snuggling close for story time.
Favorite books and whispered words.

Hello, cuddles.

Yawning wide — it's time for bed.
Gentle kiss and nighty-night.

Hello, sleepy.

Rocking at the close of day.
Evening sky and shining stars.

Hello, dreamer.

Good night, my little sweetheart—
I'm oh, so glad you're here.

Welcome to the
great, big world.

For Abigail

—Helen

SLEEPING BEAR PRESS™

2395 South Huron Parkway, Suite 200
Ann Arbor, MI 48104
www.sleepingbearpress.com

Printed and bound in the United States.

10 9 8 7 6 5 4 3 2 1

Library of Congress Cataloging-in-Publication Data

Names: James, Helen Foster, 1951- author. | Brown, Petra, illustrator.
Title: Welcome to the world / by Helen Foster James ; illustrated by Petra Brown.
Description: Ann Arbor, Michigan : Sleeping Bear Press, [2020] |
Audience: Ages 0-4. | Summary: Illustrations and easy-to-read text welcome
a new baby and celebrate the wonders shared during his or her first year,
including warm sunshine, splashing in the bath, and snuggling for story time.
Identifiers: LCCN 2020007405 | ISBN 9781534110120 (hardcover)
Subjects: CYAC: Babies—Fiction. | Parent and child—Fiction.
Classification: LCC PZ7.J154115 Wel 2020 | DDC [E]—dc23
LC record available at https://lccn.loc.gov/2020007405